Bride of the River God

SARAH A. MACKLIN

Dancing Star
Press

Bride of the River God by Sarah A. Macklin

First published by Dancing Star Press

Dancing Star Press
1222 N Grand River Ave
Lansing, MI 48906

www.dancingstarpress.com

Cover Illustration by Olusayo Ajetunmobi

ISBN: 978-1-7321418-4-1

BRIDE OF THE RIVER GOD

Anene just wanted the singing to stop. Her people's jubila-
tions rode across the surface of the river hitting her in
waves and grating against her soul. She balled her fists up,
crumpling the fine skirt her mother had made her for this
day. She lowered her head, trying to shut out the sound
with her shoulders. The thick, red beads of her headdress
swung into view as she did so and she was grateful. No one
would be able to see the tears threatening to fall. This was
all too much.

Anene tried to sit still as the six men guided her little raft
towards the center of the river. Fat bracelets of the same
precious red beads ran up her arms to the elbow and necklace after necklace weighed down on her chest. She remembered the delight in the eyes of the women of her family
as they prepared her this morning for her sacrifice. They
called it a tribute but what else could it be but a sacrifice?

She was to be the bride of the river god Nniro, the creator
of humans, deity of the river that gave life to her people.
She wrinkled her skirt further. It was a ceremony held only

once a generation and this generation it fell on her. Anene held her head up, blinking tears away. This was supposed to be an honor. She wasn't supposed to be sad. Her new home would be in the gods-world to... to please her lord and husband.

How did one even please a husband who was a god? Anene had seen her share of marriages, seen the celebrations, the happiness that came with them. She even had an idea of what went on between husband and wife. Would her new husband expect her to tend to his house? To cook and clean for him? She swallowed. Would he expect her to share his bed? Surely it would kill her. Anene shook her head vigorously, the beads of her headdress clicking together. *This was an honor*, she repeated, making herself believe it. *This was an honor.*

The men guiding her raft walked out until the waters reached their necks and set her adrift. She steadily moved toward the center of the wide river, her route taking her against the current. Anene's stomach knotted painfully and she worked to steady her breathing. A cool wind began as her raft drifted to a stop, chilling every exposed part of her. It was oddly quiet and Anene realized she couldn't hear her people anymore. She resisted the urge to look back for fear of shaming her parents with her looks of longing.

The waters around the raft began to ripple and eddy then a dozen scaled hands broke the surface. Anene bit her lip against the scream in her throat. This time she couldn't stop herself from looking back. Did they not see this? Her people seemed so far away, still singing on the river's shore swept up in their joy. The hands grabbed the raft and pulled down.

Anene didn't have the chance to give a proper scream before she was dragged underwater. All of her weight instantly left her and she felt like she was falling. She grabbed onto the lashings of the raft, fearful of floating off into the depths of the river. The hands that pulled her down belonged to women, strange blue women. They were covered in scales from head to toe, their hair trailing behind them in green curls with river plants twisted in them. One smiled at her revealing sharp, fish-like teeth. The woman reached out to her, placing a scaly finger over Anene's lips. "Breathe," she heard her say over the rushing waters.

Anene looked at the woman incredulously but her lungs demanded air. She took in a deep breath, the terror of drowning leaping up. Another breath and she was still alive. The women looked to her with reassuring smiles and she gave them a weak smile in return. If it was water she breathed it didn't feel like it at all. She took another few breaths just to calm the part of her mind that still screamed that she would drown.

The women pulled her farther down, much farther than the river would have allowed them to go. The waters around them darkened for a time, then lightened and Anene could see a grand compound below them. Their descent slowed and the women set her raft down gently in the compound's main courtyard. Anene stood, legs weak from fear, and looked up at the building before her. Great towers rose into the water, the wavy light from the tiny, distant sun playing along their walls. Bright geometric designs of inlaid shell covered every surface. Schools of fish swam by like birds, some stopping to rest near the spires. The courtyard was a beautiful garden of aquatic plants that she'd never seen in every color imaginable. Anene took a step off the raft, feeling light but not truly underwater either. She moved freely, without the sluggishness she expected. The water surrounded her like an embrace but it lacked its resistance. She took a deep breath, the thought dawning on her that this would be her new home.

The six fish women gathered before her, kneeling to the ground, foreheads touching the earth, palms turned up and extended to her. "Welcome to the home of our lord, Nniro. We are pleased to welcome his newest bride."

Anene froze at her title. She looked back up to the small disk of the sun. There truly was no way back now.

The tallest of the fish women shuffled forward on her knees, bowing again. "I am Jalao, head of our lord Nniro's servants. We will make you ready for your new husband."

The fish women rose and ushered her inside. Her sandals made barely a sound as she walked along in the midst of the attendants. They swept her along to an opulent room colored in soothing blues and purples. Her heavy necklaces and bracelets were swept away, replaced with jewelry made of shells and bright glass beads. Her skirt, that her mother had walked four days to buy the fabric for, was taken and replaced with one in all the colors of the river, a breathtaking mix of greens, blues, grays, and purples. Her headdress remained, the only piece of home they left her, to be removed by her god-husband.

Once she was dressed to their satisfaction, the women began to rub her down with a strange ointment that they said would take away the scent of the mortal world. Anene bit her lip to stop herself from bursting into tears.

The fish women looked her over, paying her compliments on her appearance and how they were sure she would make a good wife. Anene didn't respond and let them sweep her through the compound again. They stopped in front of a massive set of double doors. They reached as high as her family's home and looked to be carved from one piece of shell. Great monsters of the river fought on it, looking like they would spring out to devour her at any moment. Two of the women opened the doors and she was led into an antechamber. The tallest of the women came to her side gesturing to another pair of doors before her. "If you go through, my lady, you'll be in the inner chambers of our lord. We are not allowed to accompany you." Before she could respond, they retreated, closing the doors behind them and leaving her alone.

Anene turned toward the entrance to the river god's rooms. She fought back tears again. This was not how she thought her wedding would be. There should be dancing, a feast. Her family should be assembled to celebrate sending her off to her husband and his family. Not... nothing. Cursing the oracle that chose her, Anene placed her hands on the doors and pushed. She stepped inside meekly and dropped to the floor in a deep bow just as the fish women did. "My great lord Nniro, god of the river, lifeblood of my people, I have come to be your... your wife." She was met with silence. Anene stayed on the floor, waiting for a response from her patron deity. Still, none came.

She lifted her head an inch hoping to see feet approaching her but there was no one about. Anene cautiously sat up, looking about. "My lord Nniro?" she called. There was no response. She realized she was in a sitting room. Plush couches filled the room, light coming from glowing orbs set into the wall. On the opposite side of the room was a small hall leading to another room. Anene gathered her courage, rising to her feet.

"My lord Nniro?" she called again, walking toward the hall. She paused before entering the hall, praying she wouldn't offend him by entering deeper into his domain. The hallway led to a grand room with a large bed on the opposite wall. Windows opened to a veranda on one side, curtains moving in the current.

Anene inched into the room. The covers had been pulled to the side of the bed and she suddenly saw a foot sticking out from the far side of it. She crept closer. "My lord?" There was no movement. She moved closer to the side and gasped.

A body lay sprawled on the floor, covers tangled about his body. A thick golden substance pooled around him and Anene quickly realized it was his blood. She clasped her hand over her mouth as her eyes reached his chest. A cavity had been ripped open in it, flesh peeled up like the rinds of a melon. His eyes stared off into the distance. Anene recognized that face from the crudely carved statue back in her village. The god Nniro.

Anene screamed, running back to the main rooms of the compound. The fish women came to her side immediately.

"My lady, what is wrong?" Jalao asked her.

"He's dead." Anene's body trembled. "He's dead."

"What do you mean, my lady?" a round faced one asked in confusion.

"I walked into his bedroom and he was on the floor... dead." She finally met the fish woman's eyes. "His chest was ripped open. It was empty." She fought back the bile gathering in her throat.

"What do you mean, empty?"

"Like there was never anything there!"

A higher voiced woman broke in, breathless. "That's impossible. He was just alive. He sent us to fetch you." Tears began to flow from her eyes, dissolving into nothing by the time they reached her cheeks.

The maids fell into despair. One began to wail loudly. Questions of what they would do now and who should they tell flew about. Jalao looked to her. "My lady, are you sure his chest was completely empty?" Anene nodded. She would never forget the scene. "Then... something has stolen his heart."

Anene's breath stopped. What could cleave a god's heart from his chest? What would be powerful enough? When her breathing returned it was panicked. What would happen to the river without its god? What would happen to her people? She looked up to Jalao. "What do we do?"

"If... if the heart is returned to him, he will come back to life."

She stared at the woman. "And if... if Nniro stays dead?"

Another woman bit at her lip. "Then the river will die, my lady."

"Then we have to get it back," Anene responded immediately. There was no question about it.

The fish women exchanged nervous glances. "We are just servants, my lady," Jalao responded.

Anene felt anger before anything else. "This is your master, your lord, laying in there dead and you won't go out to try to save him?" She looked around and each of them avoided her gaze. "If the river dies, my people die. Don't you care?" They muttered excuses to her. Anene felt her face getting hot. The idea that they would leave this task to her, a mortal woman who knew nothing of the gods-world, left her outraged. She wanted to spit on each of them. Anene pulled herself up to her full height, staring them down. "Then I'll go."

♀

Fish women were useless, Anene decided. They led her to a door on the opposite side of the manor, this one with a scene of strange creatures battling carved into the rainbow-colored shell. On the other side was the path to the rest of the gods-world. She breathed in deeply, trying to steady herself.

"We wish you luck, our lady," she heard from behind her.

Anene nodded without looking back, afraid the expression on her face would kill them instantly. Another deep breath and she pushed the doors open. The path was underwhelming. Plain and simple, it led out to a field in the distance. She sighed. There were no other buildings in sight, no cities, no villages. Just the path. Wherever she ended up going it was going to be a very long walk.

Anene started her journey trying her best to ignore the dark thoughts swirling about her head. She began to shed the jewelry the fish women had burdened her with, leaving them in a trail behind her. They were unnecessary on such a long journey and she wasn't sure she wanted to attract any attention from whatever may be around. She began to take in her surroundings warily. Whatever took Nniro's heart had to be powerful and dangerous. What if she ran into it on the path? She shook her head and concentrated on the path ahead.

Strange fish swam past her as she walked, creatures with fins and too many legs. Fish with the faces of men. Little shrimp-like things with a ribbon of hair down their backs. Anene shuddered looking at them. If this was just in this part of the gods-world, she didn't want to see what other creatures could populate the rest of it. She turned her attention back to the path. Strange fish couldn't be a concern if she wanted to save the river and her people.

She walked for what seemed like hours but the sun above didn't move from its position. Perhaps time didn't flow here or maybe it just flowed slowly. A fish, as tall as she was and long enough to wrap around her six times, swam in front of her, blocking her path. She could see her reflection perfectly in its scales and her annoyed face scowled back at her. It took a moment before it passed completely and she thanked it for finally getting out of the way.

Anene took a step forward and froze as she noticed a figure beside the path ahead, waiting. She couldn't see them quite clearly. The silhouette wavered with the flow of the waters of Nniro's domain. They were tall and darkness clung to them. Was this it? Was this what took Nniro's heart? She took another step forward and they didn't move. She put a hand to her stomach. She couldn't take it tying in any more knots. Pulling on what bravery, or perhaps stubbornness, she had left, she walked forward.

As she approached the figure, their form grew clearer. The strange fish didn't come near here, as if there were a barrier. Her weight began to come back to her as well until she felt as if she walked on dry land again. Behind her she saw the path and the fish swirling just below water. She blinked, stunned at the sudden change in the landscape. Would everywhere change like this? Anene turned her attention back on the figure ahead, ready in case it wanted to strike out at her. She had no idea what she was going to do if it did but she'd have to come up with a plan. She scolded herself. *Think of something!*

The figure turned bright red eyes on her, eyes set in the face of one of the most handsome men she'd ever seen. He wore a long cloak of a gold. Black designs were scattered over it, depicting various battles. Beneath the cloak he wore only a loincloth made from the hide of some unknown animal. But what she noticed most were the sword and shield he held in his hands. Anene tried to act as if she didn't see him and walk past. The moment she reached him, his sword sliced down in front of her, barring the way.

"You," he began, his voice deep like thunder, "are a mortal."

It almost sounded like a question. "I am," she responded, struggling to keep her voice even.

"The gods-world is no place for your kind."

"I'm... I'm the new bride of Nniro."

An eyebrow raised on that beautiful, deep earthen brown face. "And why are you here? Are you trying to run away?"

Anene swallowed difficultly. There was accusation in his voice. "My lord Nniro is... dead. His heart was stolen."

The man lowered his sword. "His heart?" He paused. "Who took it?"

"I don't know. I have to find out." Her mind raced. She really didn't know where to look or what to look for. She might be searching for the rest of her life.

"You need to go to our father, Kifeaba in the Mountains of Sun and Moon." He pointed his sword ahead along a path that forked from her present one. "He will know what has happened." He turned those red eyes back to her. "But be careful. Not all will take kindly to a mortal wandering the gods-world. Some will wish to harm you. Tell them you have the permission of Usan, the guardian, to be here."

Anene bowed as low and as humbly as she could, recognizing the name. She knelt before the god who protected the entirety of the gods-world. "Thank you, great Usan. I will try to make my wanderings here short."

"Keep walking. Do not stop to rest until you reach the Mountains of Sun and Moon. Such could be the end of your journey." She blinked and he was gone. Anene rose. She had to keep moving.

ᛢ

One foot in front of the other. That was what she focused her mind on. Around her trees began to sprout up, closing in on the field she'd first entered. Flowers scattered in the tall grass bloomed and withered in time with the ripples of an unfelt wind. Insects now pestered her, flying near her ears with questions. Anene had heard tales all her life about the speaking animals of the gods-world but to actually hear them was unsettling.

"What is it?"

"It smells different. Is it from the underworld?"

"Is it evil?"

"Why is its hair so short?"

"It smells of water. Is it from the sea?"

Anene flailed her arms frantically, chasing them away. "I am a person," she shouted, her voice shaking the leaves of the few trees around. She instantly regretted raising her voice. What if she attracted the attention of something more powerful than bugs? "I am a person," she reiterated, calmer now. "Now, leave me alone."

She had a few moments of peace before they found her again. "What is a person? Is it a mortal?"

"Mortals should not be here."

Anene ground her teeth. "I am the bride of Nniro. I have the permission of Usan the gatekeeper to be here."

"Permission of Usan."

"Bride of Nniro."

"You are a great woman indeed."

"Can we help you, lady of the river?"

Her heart felt like it stopped at her new title. "Uh, no, well, yes. Am I going on the right path to the Mountains of Sun and Moon? I need to reach them as quickly as possible."

The insects flew ahead of her, forming a crude arrow. "The mountains are this way, yes, lady of the river. We will show you the way."

"Thank you," she said feeling silly talking to a swarm of flies. "Now, I wish for quiet."

They fell silent save for the buzzing of their wings. Anene wasn't sure about being led along by them, but she surely knew as much about this place as a blade of grass so she couldn't possibly be in any more danger. The trees began to grow even closer together as she walked, some shooting up to their full height in a matter of moments. The path wound its way along clearly, but she suddenly found herself in a forest instead of the field she began her journey in.

She looked behind her and saw no sign of the sprawling field. She slowed her pace. She prayed she'd be able to find her way back when all this was finished. Anene looked ahead, past the swarm of flies, and the path was clear, twisting away through the thick growth. She didn't like this one bit. The trees were even thicker now, some trunks fighting for space. She swore she saw some rubbing and straining against each other. Strange calls began to sound out from the trees and she saw the shadows of quick animals swinging through the canopy. She suddenly wished she hadn't commanded the flies to be quiet.

Birds, some with two wings, some with more, began to flutter down from high branches, tilting their heads to look at her. They chirped and clucked lowly amongst themselves. Anene kept her angry gaze on the path. She didn't appreciate being the subject of gossip even if she couldn't understand them. The birds kept up with her, but thankfully, they didn't crowd her.

She'd traveled for some time, lost in her own thoughts, before she noticed they were gone. A sigh of relief escaped her. All that noise was annoying. She looked to the flies but they'd disappeared as well. Anene almost stopped, then she remembered Usan's warning. She had to keep going. The forest had grown quiet as well. No, silent. Anene's heart sped. Something was lurking.

She prayed to every god to keep her safe from... whatever was out here. Did they have lions and leopards here? She could only imagine what sort of strange predator could be on the hunt. She quickened her pace, wanting to be done with this forest as quickly as she could.

"Little mortal woman," something purred behind her.

Anene dared look over her shoulder and bit her lip to keep from screaming. A baboon, large as a rhinoceros, lowered itself onto a massive root. It smiled at her, its mouth holding one too many sets of fangs. There was a mischievous light in its eyes that Anene didn't like. "You smell of the great river."

"That is where I came from, but if you'll excuse me. I have to be going." She quickened her pace, taking every other moment to glance behind her. She wasn't letting this... creature out of her sight. A great shadow passed over her and the baboon landed on a branch over the path ahead of her.

"Did you drown, little mortal woman?" It swung down, landing only a few feet from her.

Anene continued walking, trying her best to look unafraid. She moved to the side of the path it wasn't obstructing. "I am very alive, lord baboon."

It laughed, walking just behind her and she could see its snout just to the left of her shoulder. "Lord baboon? You honor me." Suddenly, it pressed its cold nose in the middle of her back, sniffing in loudly. "You do smell of the great river! Very much so. You've been perfumed to smell of it." The baboon bounded ahead of her and she took a step back. "You must be his newest bride."

She didn't like this monkey's smile as he said bride. "I am," she said, drawing herself up straight. "And I have a very important errand. Excuse me." She made the last statement sound more like an order, praying it would back down. It laughed at her again, turning sideways to block the path completely. Panic rose in her. Usan told her not to stop, but she couldn't keep going with this baboon in the way. "Please move," she said firmly as she neared it.

Its smile grew crueler and wider, showing all of its sharp teeth. It shot a hand out, catching her by the arm. "I've always wondered," it began pulling her in close, "what Lord Nniro sees in you mortal women." It began sniffing about her. "Especially when there are so many who'd be more than willing to... comfort him. What is it about you all that endears him so to you?" She jumped when it smelled around her rear. "Could he enjoy using you until you are useless? You don't seem one that would be much for conversation. Maybe your fleeting lives bring him entertainment?"

"Lord baboon, I have a very important errand to perform for my lord and you are keeping me from it." She stuck her chin out defiantly. "Please move out of the way."

"You intrigue me. Perhaps I will keep you here a little longer. I've never gotten to see a mortal before."

Anene tried to pull away from it, but its grip was firm. "I have Lord Usan's permission to be here. You can't do this. You can't keep me. I am the bride of Nniro."

It pressed its snout to her crotch, breathing in. "You are not his bride yet."

Anene raked her nails down the sides of its face, causing bright red cuts to pop up. The baboon's grip loosened and she dashed under its belly to run down the path. She picked up her skirts, moving as fast as she could to get away from it. Behind her, she heard its snarls as it began the chase. She knew there was no hope of outrunning it. But she had to keep going. She had to reach the mountains.

Another huge shadow passed over her and she ducked, ready for the attack. None came. The sound of fighting came from behind her. She looked back to see a jaguar rolling on the ground with the baboon. The fight was vicious between them, every bite being answered by a slash of claws. In a moment, the baboon kicked away from its attacker, running off into the forest. The jaguar turned its five red eyes on her.

Anene tried everything in her might to move, but her body disobeyed. There was no running from something like this. It walked up to her calmly and she closed her eyes, bracing for attack. Instead, she was shoved. She stumbled up the path. She looked to the great cat as she regained her footing. It walked up and pushed her along, more insistently. She had to keep moving. Anene nodded and ran, praying to be out of this forest soon.

ᛡ

The air was growing cooler. Anene rubbed her arms vigorously as she walked. The forest was thinning out, the trees growing farther and farther apart until the landscape gave way to another open area. Rocky hills came up before her, with scrubby plants clinging to life. She let out a sigh. Was there no end to this journey?

Anene looked up to the sky. The sun was still in the same position, peeking in and out from behind thick gray clouds. Had the sun even moved at all? How long had she been walking? It looked like it might rain and she prayed that it would just pass over. The flies hadn't returned after the baboon fled, but she was glad. Their chattering wouldn't do anything to lighten her mood.

The path turned to gravel, large rocks hurting her feet through her sandals. How long had she been walking? Her legs ached. All she wanted to do was slow down, or maybe even sit for just a few moments. She dragged her gaze along the side of the path. The boulders that jutted up sporadically along the path were so inviting. She remembered Usan's warning, but would it really hurt to rest for just a minute? Just one minute. She longingly eyed a large, flat rock that was at perfect stool height.

"You look tired," came a voice from farther along the path. Anene looked up. A toad perched on one of the larger boulders, like it was basking in the scant sunshine.

"I am." She slowed down even more, wary of meeting another beast so soon. As she drew closer she could see the toad easily came up to her chest. "You look sleepy as well." She hoped it was and would leave her alone.

It lazily stretched out a back leg. "I'm a little sleepy, but I always am. That is why I'm resting." It blinked slowly. "You should probably rest too."

"I... can't." She forced herself to speed up. "I have to get to the Mountains of Sun and Moon. It's very important."

"Why is it so important? What's happened that a mortal would have to make such a journey? It's so dangerous here for one of your kind." It leaped to another tall rock ahead of her. It actually looked concerned.

"I have to... find something that belongs to the god of the great river. He is... unable to find it himself."

"My word, why would he be unable to find anything of his own? Is he sick, hurt?"

Anene wasn't sure about this toad. "He's injured and cannot make the journey himself. I came instead. I'm... to be his wife."

The toad hopped down to the path, lowering itself to the ground. "The wife of Lord Nniro. I humble myself before you. You are but a mortal but you already have the presence of a goddess."

She didn't know about her presence but it was nice that it wasn't trying to harm her. "Uh, you may rise," she tried, in her most official sounding voice.

It stood with an open mouth that she assumed was a smile. "You have come such a long way by yourself. Please have a seat, my lady. I will fetch you water." It hoped off the path to a small stone that was shaped like the perfect seat. "Please, my lady, rest yourself."

"I was told not to stop."

It patted the "seat" of the rock. "How will you reach your goal if you faint from exhaustion? Have a seat, my lady. A few moments rest won't put your mission in jeopardy."

Just a few moments, she thought staring at the rock. "Not too long."

The toad smiled at her again as she sat down. "Rest yourself, my lady. All will be fine."

Anene relaxed for the first time since she was woken this morning to prepare for her marriage. Her leg muscles twitched from being so suddenly still. It was such a relief to merely sit down. She rubbed her thighs to calm them. It wouldn't matter if she took a moment to rest. It really couldn't. With all she had to endure up to now, she needed a moment to rest.

"Here you are, my lady," the toad said, presenting her with a small stone bowl filled with water with its front feet. "Drink. Regain your strength. You must have gone through a lot."

Anene drank. The water was refreshing beyond belief. She felt it trickle down her throat and the pleasing, cooling sensation spread through her entire body. "Thank you, toad."

"You are very welcome, my lady." It hopped on a rock beside her. "You must have been very excited when you were chosen to be Lord Nniro's bride. It's quite the honor."

Anene's smile wavered. "It was very much an honor."

The toad looked at her, its eyes blinking one at a time. "You do not seem very happy. It is on your face but the rest of you tells a different story. Was there another in the mortal world?"

"No!" Her face burned under the question. "There wasn't anyone. I just... didn't want to be chosen." Anene's shoulders slumped. It felt as if a weight was lifted. "This isn't the sort of life I thought I'd have. And the oracle that chooses the new bride wouldn't pick another. I know I should be honored. I know I'm supposed to be happy, but I don't want to be a god's wife. I thought my life would be normal. A normal husband and a normal family that I would become part of. I mean, eventually. I wasn't prepared for *this* and now everyone expects me to be happy and honored."

The toad nodded sagely. "You have had much put on you. If my life were to change so suddenly I don't know if I'd be able to take it as well as you, my lady. And now, this life has shoved you down a very dangerous road. It's a shame. You don't deserve this."

Anene felt the tears sting her face before she realized she was crying. "I don't. I didn't do anything to deserve this. Good or bad. I just want to go home. I just want my life back."

"And you shouldn't have to endure such, my lady. I can see you are a good and noble woman. I know you have lived a good life bringing joy and laughter to all those around you. This is a travesty. A hardship that should be put on some other woman." The toad placed a knobby hand on her knee. "What would you do if you could return to your old life?"

Anene wiped away a tear. "What?"

"What if I told you I knew of a way to return to your world, to your old life?"

"How is that possible?"

"We toads are lowly creatures. We are seldom noticed, rarely cared for. We go places, dig down to spots that no one else knows of."

She wiped the other lazy tears rolling down her cheeks. "But I can't. If I don't go, the river will die."

"The oracle will have to chose someone else and she can complete your errand. Surely your return will prove you unworthy of Lord Nniro." The toad paused as if hesitant to continue. "And perhaps unworthy of a proper marriage." It bobbed its head. "Forgive me, my lady, but you don't seem as if you're excited about the prospect of marriage to anyone. Perhaps this may be your best way out of the situation."

Anene rose slowly. A quiet far away voice was telling her to keep moving, but she was so tired. All she wanted to do was leave this world. "Please, lead the way."

ρ

"How much farther?" Anene's legs began to wobble as she struggled to keep up with the eager toad.

"Not too much farther, my lady."

Around them the rocky hills began to settle out, the earth groaning and shifting. Boulders were swallowed up and the patchy grass began to flourish again. The air warmed around them to her pleasure.

Anene sighed. Was this wise? The toad seemed like it was truthful and wanted to help her so much. It still gave her encouraging smiles as they went along. It hopped ahead of her in a steady but fast pace. At moments she had to jog to close the distance between them. The quick pace was making her even more exhausted, but for a chance to go home she'd endure the pain.

The world around her changed again, the land flattening completely. Thin, weak trees began growing up, looking exhausted from their efforts. They leaned and swayed like drunk men. Fog roamed between them in concentrated little clouds. The grass gave way to great patches of moss that squished and gave when she stepped on them. Anene's sandals were soon soaked.

"Not much farther, my lady," the toad croaked with another smile thrown back at her.

She hoped so. Traipsing around with wet feet was not her ideal way to travel. They headed toward a stand of trees that grew together like gossiping old women. As they approached, the trees parted, revealing a little clearing. In it was a tall structure made of gigantic, flat stones upended. An even larger slab lay across the top. A little light came from the opening that must have served as the door.

"Is this your home?" she asked cautiously.

"This is the home to many of my kind."

The toad led her inside and the warmth of a fire immediately filled her. She looked around to see a room far bigger than the outside suggested. Various perches and shelves held a collection of toads of all shapes, sizes, and colors. They croaked quietly, all conversations changing when they noticed her entrance. A few hopped down to welcome her, quite eagerly. Others chirped their greetings from their perches. Anene tried to accept the hospitality graciously, but it was hard to not show unease when surrounded by a knot of man-sized toads.

The toad she met on the road hopped up to a shelf, croaking loud enough to catch everyone's attention. "This is an honored guest," it announced importantly. "This is the bride of Lord Nniro and the first mortal to travel this far into the gods-world in ages." The chorus of welcomes started again and Anene felt some of her apprehension melt away. "We must bring her food and drink." A loud cacophony of croaks came from the toads and they scurried down side halls to gather a meal.

Her toad hopped back to her. "Please, my lady, have a seat." It led her to a low shelf, and she settled onto it.

"How far away is the way back to the mortal world?"

"It is not far. But you need food and drink to regain your strength." It nodded like it was agreeing with itself. "After you have had a meal, we will begin. But you must be strong enough for the journey."

Anene sighed, leaning back against the wall. She wanted to go now, to reach her home as soon as possible. She closed her eyes as she waited and she could see her parents' house as clear as if she were there. Surely her parents would welcome her back. Shouldn't they? Shouldn't her return be cause for celebration? If not for the village, at least among her family. She saw her parents welcoming her back with open arms. It didn't matter how much people would talk about her. She knew her mother and father would love her to the ends of the earth and back.

The toads reconvened in the main room bringing crude plates and bowls of foods she'd never seen before. Anene looked them over carefully, glad to see it was not bugs and worms. She took a small cup from an orange-colored toad at her left. The liquid smelled sweet and she took a sip. Her face lit up at the delightful taste. She examined the various plates until she found a food that looked relatively familiar. Taking a couple of fingerfuls of the whiteish paste, she sniffed it before placing it in her mouth. It was delicious. She took the plate from the toad, suddenly realizing how hungry she was.

The toads began croaking in excitement, encouraging her to taste from more dishes. Anene gladly obliged them. Everything they presented her with was wonderful and unlike anything she'd ever tasted, yet so familiar at the same time. Her drink was sweet like juice from the ripest fruits. This was better than any feast at home.

She was on her third plate when she noticed the toads looking at her differently than before. Then a thick drop landed on her shoulder. She looked up to see one of the toads settling back into his perch innocently, his mouth wet with saliva. Her attention snapped back to the toads presenting her with plates. A few of their lips were wet as well. The others looked at her like a dog waiting for scraps. Her heart thundered. She moved to get up, but the toad who brought her rushed up amongst his comrades.

"No, my lady," it almost shouted. "Rest yourself."

Anene scooted to the edge of her seat. "I think we should

be on our way."

"No!"

Fear lanced her and she jumped out of the seat. The toads rushed in, their dogpile keeping them from getting a good hold on her. She jumped back up on her shelf, leaping to the next perch. A toad reached for her from above, and she slapped away its hands with all her strength. Another shot its tongue out, catching her ankle. She slammed her fist down on it before she could fall, freeing herself. Another pair of jumps and she reached the floor just as the majority of toads dislodged themselves from the cluster.

A large one, black with orange spots, leapt in front of her, barring her escape. "We have been forbidden to eat mortals for many eons. It's been so long. So long."

The toads approached behind her, their tongues lolling out of their mouths. She turned suddenly on the toad blocking her way, punching it in the eye, her hand pushing the orb down into its head. As it struggled to pop its eye back out she kicked it in the chin, snapping its mouth shut on its tongue. The toads behind her started to lash out at her. She scrambled out of the way, shoving past the large black one and running out of the doorway.

Mud sucked at her feet, claiming a sandal in her flight. Toad calls grew into a cacophony behind her. She spared a glance back to see the mass of toads pouring from the entrance of their home. She pushed herself to run faster. Anene jumped over a small boulder, skidding down into a small valley. A shadow engulfed her as a toad landed on the rock she'd just jumped from. She screamed, heading into the spindly trees. She didn't bother to look back now. The sounds of the toads' approach were steady, their great webbed feet slapping down on the wet grass.

Fog began to close in densely around the forest, blocking out even the sun. The trees reached up and disappeared into the low clouds. Anene's body burned but she ran despite it. The toads croaked to each other, the sounds spread out over the forest. She stopped for a moment beside the thickest tree she could find and turned around. Eerie shapes hopped through the fog, but surely they were just as blinded as she was. Anene took a deep breath, filling her burning lungs. A moment passed and the fog parted when the big black toad hopped into view. It saw her clearly, sending up a strangled cry of rage. Her legs shook as she started to run again and every step was a struggle.

The forest floor upturned sharply, drying out with rocks dislodging as she ran. The toad behind her had a harder time with it. She could hear it slipping and struggling. The steep hill plateaued with tree roots sticking up as if they were trying to trip her. Anene hopped and stumbled over them, terror driving her every move. The fog thickened around her and suddenly she found her feet in midair.

She fell, screaming, her back scraping against outcroppings on the cliff. She landed roughly in a muddy pond. Plants slid across her skin in a sickening caress. Anene looked above her to the top of the cliff. It was just a dark shape in the distance. She swallowed the shriek in her throat when the looming shape of the toad came to the edge. Anene scrambled to get to her feet, half swimming to hide against the cliff. The mud clung to her shoulders threatening to pull her in. She held her breath and nearly felt as if time stopped with it as she waited for the toad to move. It made a couple of croaks, looking around, then moved from the edge.

Anene held her breath until she couldn't bear it anymore. She moved through the muck until her feet reached solid ground again. Cold settled in with the fog. Tears started to flow now that her fear leeched away. She'd lost the path. Around her the trees showed no sign of parting to any other terrain. She wiped the mud from her face. All she could do was keep walking.

♀

Fog sat like an unwelcome houseguest. Anene reached down for her remaining sandal, tossing it off into the forest. How long had she been walking? It felt like an eternity. Her left foot hurt from hours of walking on the uneven ground. It only seemed fitting that her right should join it. The tall, thin trees around her swayed to a secret rhythm. Their trunks moved in and out of visibility, haunting the edges of her vision.

Anene rubbed her arms against the chill that wouldn't seem to leave her. Half-dry mud smeared up and down her arms adding to her misery. She was hopelessly lost in a forest that seemed to go on forever. Her heart was a stone in her chest. What if it never ended? Would she wander around until she died from thirst or hunger? Perhaps from exhaustion. Maybe the toads would find her, or something worse, at her weakest and make a meal out of her.

Anene continued walking, her legs moving without thought. The trees creaked in familiar tones, the highs and lows of conversation. The hushed sounds of aunties disapproving just beyond your hearing. She hunched her shoulders in, trying to shut out the noise. Even though there wasn't a word spoken, she still felt the weight of the sound.

She wandered through the fog until another sound pierced the creaking. Anene slowed her walk. She looked around the forest until a dark shape became clear in the fog. She took another step forward, not wanting to get closer but needing to see what this new visitor was. "W-who's there?" Her voice trembled more than she wanted.

The fog thinned and she could see the shape of a large leopard. It turned toward her and after a moment five red eyes opened. Anene froze as the enormous cat from the jungle stared her in the eyes. It blinked slowly, unmoving. She swallowed, unsure of what to do in this creature's presence. It helped her before, but would it help her again? The leopard blinked again then narrowed its eyes at her. A moment after, it walked away. Anene stared, mouth hanging open. She was alone again. Fat, hot tears streaked down her cheeks, making stripes in the dirt on her face.

At her first choked sob of despair, the leopard stopped, looking back. Anene felt a minute sliver of hope leap up in her. It shook its head and walked toward her. Stopping once again, it turned and motioned with its head. The sliver of hope grew. She scrambled to catch up as it walked off.

The leopard glanced back at her occasionally while they traveled. Anene felt the displeasure pouring off of it. She wanted to say something, thank you, anything at all, but its glares told of the desire for silence. The fog began to lift as they continued, melting away under the growing sunshine. The chattering auntie trees shrunk, thinning out to make way for grasslands. The grass sprung up soft beneath her feet. It continued to grow up until it reached her knees.

Anene glanced aside sheepishly. She knew she looked hideous, pitiful. Covered in dirt and mud and filth, she could only imagine what the leopard thought of her now. She opened her mouth to apologize to the feline.

"You are a selfish woman," it said before anything could leave her. She fumbled for a response. "Selfish and spoiled."

"No, I'm not."

"Aren't you?" it snapped back. "You were told not to stop. For anything. At the first opportunity you abandoned your mission. Selfish. And spoiled."

"I am not," Anene protested again.

"Then how did you end up in the toad marsh? Were you not seduced by its words?"

"I didn't want this. I didn't want any of this." She tried to stop herself from crying again, but lazy tears escaped. "I didn't ask to be Nniro's bride and I surely didn't ask to be on this mission."

"Was there someone else who would do it in your place?"

Anene thought to the attendants back in the underwater palace. "No, none."

"Then it falls to you."

"That's not fair."

"Life isn't fair."

She scowled at the leopard. "Why couldn't the other gods find his killer?"

"The ways of the gods are not the ways of mortals. Each god has their own domain and does not meddle in each other's affairs. Their gaze is on their own holdings, save the king, and if he has not interfered then he has good reason. That is why you must go to him." The leopard glanced back. "He should be able to see where Lord Nniro's heart is. Then you will be able to return it to him." It paused. "Sometimes burdens are placed on our shoulders, heavy burdens that seem like more than we will ever be able to carry. It is then that we may find strength that we wouldn't have found before."

Anene nodded absently, letting the leopard's words sink in. Strong was the last word she would use for how she felt right now. Her eyes slid around the landscape, searching for something to focus on rather than her hopelessness. She watched tall beasts with six thick legs feast on grass as they walked by. The leopard was right, she thought as her mind finally settled. This was, unfortunately, her burden to carry. That didn't make it any less of a nightmare.

"What will you do once you retrieve the heart?" the cat asked, its tone softening.

She blinked. "I... I'll take it back to Lord Nniro."

"And after that?"

"I will become his bride."

Silence passed between them again. "You are doing an incredible feat, a mortal bringing a god back to life. He'll owe you a great debt." The leopard looked back at her pointedly. "Perhaps you should remember that."

Anene nodded slowly, unsure of how to respond. "Who are you? Are you a god?"

"Yes... and no." Silence. "I am... part of a god."

The leopard glanced back again and the particular intensity in its five eyes sparked a thought. "Are you Usan the gatekeeper?

"Yes, and no."

"Why are you helping me?" she asked at last.

"You move outside the restraints of your people. That is something I understand."

Anene followed obediently, a myriad of thoughts swirling in her head. Nniro owing her a debt rose to the top. Could she possibly ask to not be his bride, to actually go home? Would he even honor such a debt to a mere mortal woman? Anene worried her lip. He had to. The gods were honorable. He had to honor all that she'd done for him.

They continued to travel until mountains grew far in the distance. Anene found herself smiling. "Are those the mountains of Sun and Moon?" she asked.

"Yes."

They climbed a small rise and Anene realized they were on the path again. The leopard sat, waiting for her to catch up to it. The mountains were a ribbon on the horizon, stretching as far as one could see in either direction. They pierced the very sky and it seemed as if the clouds were afraid to touch them. The leopard turned its five eyes upon her. "Stay on the path and all will be fine. Keep moving and let no one intimidate you. You have every right to come here."

"Thank you," Anene said as humbly as she could. The great cat nodded and bounded into the grass. She looked up the path to the distant mountains. She took a deep breath, steeling herself. All she had to do was make it to the mountains and half her trek would be over.

♀

Anene jumped as a rock tore itself free from beside the path and rolled away. The grass began to wither and die as she watched, giving way to parched land that blackened and split beneath the shadowy sky. Red light spilled from the fissures, the heat wavering in the air. Anene jumped with every snap as new cracks rent the ground. Spindly trees shot up, their fingers stabbing toward the sky. White bark clung to trunks that looked like they'd snap at any moment. The trees groaned and howled as she passed, cries that spoke of a tortured existence. She tried to ignore them, but their song was the only sound in this hot, dead landscape. In the middle distance, she could make out low creatures shuffling along the ground, unbothered by the heat rising. A pair of hunched over animals rooted through the dirt, their quills and scales quivering as they worked.

In front of her a great haze obscured the distance, blocking out much of the path and the world. The sun was a blurry dot behind dark clouds, but she could still see her goal. The mountains of Sun and Moon peeked out above the haze, the tops of the highest peaks defiantly piercing through. Anene focused on the path ahead, ignoring more rocks that rolled away from her approach.

"What is that smell?"

Anene spun around at the voice. She searched the area, the haze thinning just enough to take in more of her surroundings. A woman, or at least they were womanlyshaped, lounged in the pale branches of a nearby tree. Her wrinkled, upturned nose sniffled the air. Wide, bat-like wings hung down from her arms. The bat-woman's gaze came to a rest on her. "Is that you?"

"I'm... sorry?" Anene stammered backing away.

In a blink, the bat-woman flapped her wings, taking off and landing in front of her. Anene cringed as she began sniffing her person. "That is you! You smell strange. Of the river. Of something else." She recoiled. "Ew, of mud and filth too." She took a moment to step back and Anene took that moment to make a little more distance between them. "Are you a mortal?"

"I am. I am the bride of Nniro and I'm on a very important mission." She took another step back. She'd had quite enough of the gods-world's inhabitants.

"You are going to the mountains, aren't you?" An amused smirk stretched the woman's lips.

"Yes, yes I am. Now, I truly need to be going." Praying that this strange bat-woman would leave her be, she turned and continued down the path.

"You'll never make it," the woman laughed after a few moments. Anene ignored her and continued. She'd had enough of traps and strange commentary. "I mean it. You'll never make it as you are."

"Well, I've made it just fine on my own so far, so good day to you, Lady Bat."

She laughed heartily. "Do you hear that, Tifirah?" she shouted into the landscape. Anene quickly looked around to see if another person or animal had sneaked up on her but saw nothing but the shuffling creatures in the distance. The bat-woman closed in on her again. "You are covered in mud from the toad forest. They tried to eat you, didn't they? Did you manage to fight your way out or did you run?"

Anene looked away from her, unable to find the words to lie. "I ran."

"You're on a 'very important mission' and you ran from toads." She laughed again, then took off to land in another tree. "I was right. You'll never make it as you are."

"Nsisi, you're confusing her."

Anene scanned the area, looking for the source of this new voice. More rocks rolled away and more trees groaned. Then she noticed one of the creatures had made its way closer to the path. It was the size of a boar and kicked up a cloud of dust as it walked. The unmistakable quills of a porcupine rose from its hunched over back. Anene cursed her luck. Why was the gods-world full of talking creatures?

It shuffled its way closer and began to grow, no, rise up. Soon a woman with a porcupine cloak stepped onto the path. Her face was kind, with scar markings on each cheek. A pair of long, white-tipped quills were stuck into her twisted hair, behind an ear. Her arms and legs were made of taut muscle, like the thickest braided rope, and in one of her hands she held a spear. She regarded Anene with a patient smile. "Nsisi tends to speak her thoughts without considering her audience. But she is right. You will not make it on your journey. Not as you are."

"Who are you?" Anene asked, looking at the long spear point.

The porcupine cloaked warrior bowed shallowly. "I am Tifirah, the First Warrior. This is Nsisi, the Apprentice. If your mission is taking you into the mountains, then you will need more to make it."

"Why do you keep saying that?" Anene was starting to tire of their riddles. "Are the mountains so dangerous? If that's the case then I should just give up now," she snapped.

Nsisi laughed again, landing on the path. "And that is

why you will not make it." She stepped up to Anene quickly, striking her in the chest with the flat of her palm. Anene staggered back, triggering another laugh from the bat-woman. "You have no fire."

Tifirah caught her wrist to steady her. "What is your name, mortal?"

"Anene," she answered attempting to pull away but found the woman's grip too strong.

"And what is your mission?"

"I have to go to the mountains of Sun and Moon. It's a very important errand for Lord Nniro." She hesitated. "I'm his bride."

The two women looked to each other then turned back to her. Tifirah shook her head. "Then it is good that your path brings you to us. You will have to learn."

"Learn what?" Anene asked as her wrist was released.

Nsisi came near her again. "To have fire. You are weak. You are timid. You are a mouse in the night, frightened of every sound, every bit of movement at the corner of your eye. There is no fire in you. Only cold, weak, fear."

"I am not weak," she snapped at them, louder than she intended. Tears began to form in her eyes. "I've been chased and almost eaten. I have been lost in the gods-world with no hope. This morning I was woken up to be cast out to become the wife of a god. I was not ever given a choice in this. So, yes, I am terrified and timid, but am I wrong to be when so much has happened to me?"

Tifirah smiled at her. "Perhaps there is a fire in you after all." She tapped Anene in the center of the chest. "That fire is what you need to ascend the mountains, but I fear you will need more." She looked off toward the peaks jutting out from behind the haze. The quills on her cloak quivered. "There are storms coming. Nsisi!" she called.

Anene watched the bat-woman warily as she snapped a branch from one of the bleached trees. She ran a hand along it and it straightened out to a simple staff. Nsisi handed it to her. Anene looked to the First Warrior in confusion. "What do you want me to do with this?"

Tifirah took a position with her spear. "Learn to fight, I hope."

"And kindle a true fire within you," Nsisi added.

Anene held the staff in front of her in what she hoped was a fighting position. Tifirah swiftly knocked it out of her hands. "No," she chided. "Try again and hold it as if you believe you will defend yourself."

Anene picked up the staff, ignoring the tingling in her fingers. "But I was told by Usan to not stop."

Tifirah glanced to Nsisi with a smirk. "He will understand. Now try again." She took a position, stronger this time, just in time to stop Tifirah's blow. The warrior smiled. "Good. Again."

They continued a slow rhythm, Tifirah teaching her the slow dance of staff fighting. Nsisi called out encouragement from the side of the path, telling her to remember her fire. Anene's hands tingled from the blows but she knew the woman whose title was the First Warrior could have dealt her even stronger ones at any time. She wasn't sure if she was getting any better but Tifirah seemed pleased as they worked.

They picked up their pace and Anene noticed movement in the corner of her eyes. She took a chance to glance aside and saw the five-eyed leopard watching from a distance.

"Usan's eyes are on you. Why would that be?" the warrior asked, glancing toward the cat.

"I... don't know." Anene glanced back at the leopard and it moved on.

Tifirah's face turned thoughtful and she began striking harder. Anene had trouble keeping up, her fingers getting hit in the process. She almost protested but saw Nsisi's smug smile and kept it to herself. She tried to attack back, unsuccessfully at first, but finally getting in strikes that forced Tifirah to defend. "Good," the warrior shouted. "Now, fight me! Do not be afraid!"

Anene gave into the surge of bravery she felt, emboldened by Tifirah's encouragement. She moved the staff as best she could, taking every opportunity to make a strike. She stepped on toes and attempted to kick at her teacher's knees. This produced encouraging laughs from both women.

As the lesson wore on, she felt no sweat on her brow or felt any fatigue. If anything, she felt more confidence as she fought. Anene noticed a familiar shape and saw the jaguar watching again. The next thing she realized, her feet were swept from beneath her and she landed roughly on the hot path. She laid there for a moment, trying to catch the breath that had been knocked out of her. Tifirah stood over her. "Keep your eyes on your goal, mortal Anene."

Anene took her offered hand, coming to her feet. She took her battle stance again but Tifirah raised a hand. "That's enough. You must continue on." She looked to the leopard who paced between two trees. "I see we have kept you long enough."

Nsisi came up to Anene, taking the staff and placing her palm over her heart. "I feel it now. And it grows stronger." She smirked. "You may make it after all."

Anene smiled back at her. "I will make it."

Tifirah nodded. "Now go. And let nothing, *nothing* deter you from your mission."

Anene bowed lowly. "Thank you," she said, feeling tears starting again.

"No tears!" Nsisi shouted.

She nodded and turned around on the path. She began walking, the haze starting to part, the great mountains becoming clearer. They suddenly looked larger to her now, as if they were attainable. Anene quickened her pace, feeling a surge of energy like a flame growing inside of her.

?

The mountains grew ever closer and Anene's pace hadn't slowed. All the aches and pains she felt before had long ago disappeared. Training with Tifirah left her feeling renewed. A small laugh escaped her as two birds flew past her in amazing acrobatic displays. She was closer to her goal, nearer to the end of this strange journey. Each step brought her a bit more hope.

She continued watching the birds flying until a large shadow flew over her. She turned to see what had flown over but couldn't find the animal. "You are disgusting," came a voice from behind her.

Anene spun, fear of the toads or the baboon lancing her. A man stood in the path staring at her with his nose turned slightly up. He wore feathers in his long, braided hair and was covered in a feathered cloak that reached his shins. It was a beautiful cloak, the feathers blending from black to white to blue. A vibrant red tipped the edge of feathers here and there. But Anene's gaze was drawn to his eyes. They were a deep blue-black. And lightning streaked within them.

He tilted his head, his eyes studying her. "I told my lady there was a mortal roaming our realm but she didn't believe me. I didn't realize you would be such a... sight up close."

Anene was suddenly aware of herself. Still covered in dried mud she must have looked hideous. "I'm sorry to have offended you with my appearance," she said carefully. "May I ask who you are? And who is your lady?"

"I am Obokei. I serve Sabako, the incomparable goddess of storms. She will be most interested in you. What is your name, mortal?"

She hesitated. "I am the bride of Nniro."

Obokei bowed and Anene had the distinct feeling of mockery. "I am honored to meet one of his many mortal brides. You must find great pleasure in your new marriage."

"I... do."

"What brings you to the keep of Lord Kifeaba? Has Lord Nniro sent you on an errand?"

Anene backed a step away. Her heart was unsure of this strange man. His eyes told of ulterior motives behind the lazy streaks of lightning. "Yes, I need to deliver a message to Lord Kifeaba."

"I could deliver it for you," he jumped in eagerly. "You've already traveled so far. I could fly ahead and deliver it to our king so that you could return to your husband's side."

She bit her lip. Did everything here want to trick or eat her? "No," she said with her brightest smile. "My lord gave me instructions to not give the message to anyone by Lord Kifeaba himself. I thank you for your kindness."

His eyes narrowed for the barest moment, a bright flash of light cutting across them. "Then at least let me fly ahead and announce your arrival."

"Very well," she said, trying to sound her best like the happy wife of a god, or at least what she thought one would sound like. "Thank you." He gave his mocking bow again then took off into the skies. Anene released a breath. She looked to the mountains again. She couldn't let anything else stop her.

The mountains grew closer with each step, faster than would be possible in the mortal world. She reached the foothills where boulders sat upright, pointing up towards the peaks. The grasses around her seemed to bow down. A pair of boulders marked the sides of the path ahead, reaching as high as six of her, and in front of them were a pair of warriors. A man and woman, taller that any mortal, stood stock still, swords at their sides. They wore matching long loincloths, with the sun and moon chasing each other. Thick beaded belts circled their torsos in a collection of bright colors.

They turned piercing brown eyes on her. Scarring in an intricate design on their foreheads made them seem even more fierce. "What is your business here?" they asked in unison.

Anene stopped, pulling herself up to her full height. "I must speak to Lord Kifeaba. It's urgent."

"We'll decide if it's urgent. Who are you?" They leaned down from their incredible height to scrutinize her.

"My name is Anene. I'm the new bride of Lord Nniro."

"You don't look like any sort of bride."

She kept her groan inside. Were all the residents of the gods-world so infuriating? "I... have had a very hard journey here. May I pass? I have the permission of Lord Usan to be here."

"Lord Usan has authority over the greater gods-world, but this is the domain of the king of all gods." They leaned in further, their faces as long as her chest. "You still haven't told us what your business is here. And don't lie. We can tell."

Anene winced as she felt their presence press down on her. Fear in her responded and she struggled to push it back down. "My lord is dead, his heart ripped out. Lord Kifeaba may have seen who did it and where the heart may be. I have to save Lord Nniro... and my people."

The man snorted derisively and the woman sucked her teeth. "What if the heart has been eaten? You've made your journey for nothing."

Instead of fear, anger swelled within her. "What will your king think, that you care so little about one of his children?" They seemed unmoved and her anger burned hotter, pushing back their heavy presence. "While you keep me here, uncaring about one of the great gods of this world, something could be eating his heart. Then his death will be on your hands."

The pair of guards pulled back, wincing. They looked to each other, turned and gestured toward the mountains. "Please go ahead."

She nodded curtly at them, passing by without another word. She was the bride of Nniro. One would think that would get some respect.

ᕯ

A rainbow rose above the palace of Sun and Moon. The light played across the large courtyard before the entrance. Birds with long opal-colored tails wandered across the grass, pecking at the ground. Gods milled about, chatting, flirting, going about like people in an average village. Anene climbed the last stair in awe of her surroundings. The palace was beautiful, with walls of a light blue stone. It almost looked like it reflected the sky.

The gods milling about stopped, staring at the intruder into the most sacred domain in all the gods-world. Anene remembered to keep her head held high. She had a mission to finish and she'd gone through too much to let their stares deter her. Even the birds watched her pass. She continued to the doors of the palace, pressing on the cool wood. They gave easily and she closed them, putting a much-needed barrier between herself and the nosy deities.

Anene found herself in a long hallway. The roof was open to the sky. The sun shined down brightly and she felt a pleasant heat. Attendants lined the hall, one at every doorway leading off. Anene found her nerve wavering. Timidly, she came to the nearest servant, a woman with skin the color of an overcast day. Her hair was cut short to her scalp and white, but still with tight curls like the girls of her village. "Excuse me." The woman looked over, thankfully with a smile. "Is this the way to see Lord Kifeaba?"

"Yes," the woman replied, her voice relaxing. "We have been expecting you."

Anene followed the woman down the hallway, glancing at the other servants and down each side hall. Each way lead to a different colonnade and courtyard. Some of them were bathed in the light of the brightest day. Others seemed to be a golden afternoon, while others were at night. Anene didn't even notice when they arrived at the end of the hallway. She stopped herself just before a collision. The door before them was carved from stone, with one side a lively daytime scene and the other a nightscape with all of its respective creatures. The cloudy-skinned servant raised a hand and the massive door began to swing open. She looked down to Anene with that relaxing smile again. "Lord Kifeaba, is ahead. I hope he can grant your desire."

Anene meekly thanked her, stepping into the room. Around the wings of the space other gods waited in attendance. Some, she knew immediately from her mother and grandmother's stories. Others, she had to guess at their identity. They spoke passionately to each other. Deciding the fate of the world and their domains, she assumed. She stepped further in and saw Kifeaba. She forgot all decorum at the sight of him. He stood on a massive platform, looking out, it seemed, to the world and beyond. His eyes were mismatched, one holding all the brightness of the sun and its twin shining with cold moonlight. The cloth wrapped about him was all the colors of sunrise. Drawings of animals played across it, shifting their placement as she stared. In his hand, he held a cane, thicker and better carved than any noble's, a wide-bodied serpent chasing its own tail. Behind that grand sight was the same serpent. It looked down at her, ripples passing over its rainbow-colored scales.

Anene snapped herself out of her stupor and dropped to the floor. "Great Lord Kifeaba, king of all gods. I've come to you to ask for your help." She waited, breath held for his response.

"What would bring a mortal girl all the way to this palace?" All the gods quieted when he spoke. His voice was a stiff wind coming off the mountain. The touch of it raised goosebumps on her skin.

"I have come to you because my Lord Nniro has been killed. On the day that I should have become his bride, I found him with his chest ripped open and his heart missing." She waited for some sort of reaction but heard none. Were they really so callous? "You see far and know much. I came hoping you saw what sort of creature attacked my lord and where it has taken his heart."

There was silence again. Anene lifted her head just enough to see the feet of everyone in the room. Not a single one stirred. She held her breath. Would they let her stay down here forever?

"I did not see when he was killed. My gaze was elsewhere. But I did see who took his heart and it was no creature."

Silence again. "Who was it, my great lord?" She tried to keep the impatience out of her voice but was doing a poor job of it.

"It was his daughter, Sabako."

Anene's head shot up despite herself. The goddess of storms? That birdman's master? "Why would she do such a thing?"

"That I cannot tell you."

Kifeaba didn't seem inclined to continue so she pressed him. "Does she still have his heart?"

"Yes."

"Where is she? I'll get it back from her."

A god to her left laughed. "How will you, a mortal girl, wrench his heart from the goddess of storms?"

"Father," started a goddess to her right, "if Nniro is dead then this girl has no place here. We should send her back to the mortal plane."

Another god covered his nose. "Please send her back. Her appearance offends me."

Anene knelt, taken back. "He is your brother," she breathed out. She looked to Kifeaba. "He is your son. He is the river itself. My people need him."

Kifeaba still didn't look directly at her. "The river will continue even with Nniro dead," he said.

"But the bounty of it will surely die with him."

"Yes, it will."

Her mouth worked, trying to make the words come out. "But my people will die."

"Yes, they will." He finally rested his eyes on her and Anene found she couldn't meet them. "Your people will not be the first to die out and they will not be the last."

Tears began to well in her eyes. All of her life she'd been taught that the gods were looking on the world with care. Now, to see them, they were cold-hearted. "How can you all care so little? How can family mean so little to you? Don't you care about anything? If this were your domains, would you care then?" A few of the surrounding deities stiffened. "If it were the mountain or war or metalwork, would you care? My people are my domain. The river is the life of my people and I will do anything for them to continue and prosper."

Anene dissolved into sobs as murmuring started around her. She didn't care if Kifeaba cast her off the mountain. It would be better than to watch her people die.

The king of the gods' voice washed over her again. "Nniro cared greatly for his creations. He wanted them to prosper and so I will respect his wishes. You will find Sabako in her keep." He motioned to his right and she could see in her mind a high mountain covered in storm clouds.

She wiped the tears from her eyes and tried to calm her sobs. "Can't you command her to return it?"

"That is a dispute between father and daughter. It is not even my place to interfere."

Anene nodded in acceptance despite her feelings. "Thank you, my great lord."

Kifeaba looked past her and a servant came up. "Give her the chance to clean herself and ready her for her journey."

She nodded, helping Anene from the floor. Anene thanked the king of the gods again and left the room.

ꝑ

A warm wind caressed Anene's freshly washed face. She had a new skirt in the richest purple, new sandals, and new gold bracelets. The servant standing beside her on the mountain path handed her a walking staff that was painted with fearsome creatures. "This path will take you directly to Sabako's keep. There should be no trouble, but please, be careful of the edge."

Anene looked a few feet to her left and the jagged rocks leading down to the ground so far below them. She nodded. "I'll be careful."

"And eat this. It will give you strength. You will need it, for Sabako's mountain is high and unforgiving." She held out a fruit Anene had never seen before. It was perfectly round and colored purple and orange. Anene took it, biting into it cautiously. An indescribable flavor flooded her mouth. Her stomach cried out for more and she devoured the sweet orange flesh. The servant laughed. "Good journey," she said, then returned to the palace.

Many-winged birds called down to her as she began her journey, sounding like children showing off. She watched them sparingly, wanting to keep her eyes on the path. It was smooth and well worn. For that, she was thankful. On the other hand, the steep drop to her left was something she could do without. The path began to meander across the mountain, zig-zagging up a sheer face and through massive sheets of rocks that caused the path to become more of a hall. The wind ripped through these passages, threatening to take her skirt from her. The birds still called to her so she obliged them with a wave. They laughed back jovially. At least they were keeping her company.

Once she was past Kifeaba's mountain, more animals appeared. Thick-wooled goats, or something close to a goat, stalked the rocks. Their legs were long and spindly, their heads oddly shaped. She watched one staring at a little lizard with blue spots on a rock ahead of it. The goat-thing stood perfectly still, staring, and Anene found herself staring with it. Suddenly, its tongue lashed out, catching the lizard and sucking it into its mouth. She cringed at the loud crunch as it began chewing. Anene inched past it. It was probably best to move on.

She walked around a bend in the path and a flash of light in the corner of her eye caught her attention. The mountain she had been shown in her mind was now in the distance. Black storm clouds churned around its summit, throwing out wide bolts of lightning. Thunder rumbled through the air and ground. It would be a dangerous walk to the top. Anene took a deep breath. It had to be done.

She walked through a small valley, watching a few of the blue-dotted lizards chase insects. Their almost frantic hunt cheered her up a bit as she rounded another bend in the path and stopped short. Her way was blocked by the feathered Obokei. He smiled in that false way of his. She thought it would be better suited on a snake; he only lacked fangs.

"You continued beyond Lord Kifeaba's palace. I applaud you. I thought you would have turned around."

Anene grasped the staff tighter. "I've come to realize I'm not so fragile."

"A sensible woman would have turned around. The path is dangerous."

"My mission is more important than anything."

The lightning played across his eyes more frequently. "Unfortunately, I won't let you finish it. My lady took Lord Nniro's heart. It belongs to her and only her."

"You knew who I was before I told you, didn't you?" She fought the urge to back away from him. She wouldn't give him any ground. "You knew why I was here."

"Of course I did, you inept little mortal. I tried to just dissuade you from continuing, but your people have always been stubborn and insipid. It seems as if you're the most stubborn of them all." The feathers of his cloak began to stand on end with small arcs of lightning racing between them. "So now I'll relieve you of your mission and my mistress will be rid of Nniro's most pesky bride."

"You can't do this," Anene objected. "Lord Kifeaba approves of this. He's honoring Lord Nniro's love of his mortals. You can't do this! You'll be punished!"

He chuckled, a laugh devoid of any mirth. "My love for my lady is greater than any fear I have of Kifeaba."

He raised his hand, lightning crackling around his fingers and lunged for her. Anene jumped to the side, throwing herself against the rocks. Obokei turned, slashing out at her with his lightning-laced fingers. She tried to turn but he caught her with a glancing blow on the shoulder. She screamed in pain and swung her staff wildly. The crack of it hitting his jaw echoed off the mountainside. He stumbled away a few feet, touching his face in disbelief. "Impossible," he breathed. "You're just a mortal. You can't possibly hurt me."

She readied her staff to swing again. "I can and I will!"

Howling with anger he flew towards her, arms outstretched. Anene swung with all of her might, hitting one of his elbows. She screamed as his other arm slashed her across the forearm, burning and cutting at the same time. She swung again and again, in panic and anger. Who was he to keep her here? He had no right to do this. Obokei caught the staff mid-swing, sneering at her in triumph. She planted her heel into his groin in reply. He tried to hold onto her staff while hunched over in pain, but she jerked it from his grasp. She swung for the side of his head. Just as she connected, his mantle flared, lightning striking out.

It hurt. Anene's arms numbed, but she still made contact. Obokei hit the ground while she was knocked back. Anene cried out as she fell down. Her breath came raggedly, her heart beating in an odd rhythm. She sat up, seeing Obokei struggling to gain his footing. She couldn't let him get the upper hand again. She couldn't let him win. Anene struggled to her feet, grasping the staff in both hands. He saw her coming and puffed up his cloak with lightning again. She didn't care. She cried out, swinging the staff down with every last bit of strength she had. The crack rang through the passage, sending birds to flight. She didn't wait for him to retaliate. She kept attacking, the staff striking him around the shoulders, the head, the hands when he tried to protect himself. She attacked him until she was winded, finally backing away.

Anene waited, slumping against the mountainside. His golden blood, not quite as brilliant as Nniro's, stained his cloak. He made noises, nothing sounding like true speech, but he didn't move against her. He barely moved at all. After another few moments, she slowly inched away from him, then hurried down the path as fast as her aching body would take her. Anene tore a piece from her skirt to make bandages for her cuts. Her eyes traveled up to the storm-covered mountain still ahead of her. There was still much she had to endure, but she would do it.

𝄞

Anene stopped short in front of the wall of rain surrounding Sabako's mountain. She looked up to the summit and the churning clouds blocking out the sun. The storm goddess's stronghold was a spear of stone, standing in competition with the rest of the sacred mountain range. Surely it was as tall as Kifeaba's peak. Clouds clung to the top, pouring their contents angrily down on the path ahead. She sighed, taking the first step into the deluge. Fat raindrops pelted her, soaking her immediately. Rivulets ran down from her hair, dulling her sight. Her skirt soon clung to her legs like a second skin. Anene trudged on.

The path turned vertical, leading up the mountain's face. She took another piece from her skirt, using it to tie her staff to her back. Finding a solid foothold, she took the first step of her climb. Rain beat against her face as she looked up for the next hand hold. She'd never climbed a mountain before. Her mother had stopped her from climbing trees when she was a girl, but as Usan said, she was finding strength she didn't know she had.

A strong gust of wind pushed down from the top of the mountain, threatening to blow her off. Anene pulled herself flat against the rocks until the wind passed. She pulled herself up farther, finding a ledge to climb to. A small path led up. Her footing would be narrow, but at least she wouldn't have to climb for a moment. The rain pelted her harder when she set foot on the path. She lost her balance, but caught herself on a nearby rock. She looked up at the summit in anger.

"You are not welcome here," came a voice on the wind.

Anene rushed up to the end of the path lest another burst of rain try to knock her down. She found purchase for her hands, planting herself against the mountainside. "I've come for Lord Nniro's heart," she shouted against the tempest. "Please call off your storm."

She was answered with another gust of wind. Anene reached up blindly, searching for a firm grip before pulling herself up. Small rocks skipped down the mountain, dislodged by the strong rain. They bounced off her exposed skin, leaving little cuts in their wake. She ignored the protests of her fingers and toes and pushed herself up.

The rain lessened, the wind increasing in its place. It chilled her wet skin, sending a shiver through her body. She gritted her teeth, climbing farther up the mountain. She found another ledge and took a moment to rest, trying to rub warmth into her cold arms. The wind buffeted her from both sides, but she held to the mountain for dear life.

"You have no right to be here," came the roaring voice again.

Anene stooped down, curling into a ball against the rocks. "I have every right to be here!" She waited another moment for the wind to stop. "I am the bride of Nniro and I will return his heart back to him."

The rains started again. Anene frowned at this display. This was ridiculous. Sabako should just give up. She would not be pushed from the mountain. She started climbing again, getting used to the exertion of it. She began to find hand- and footholds easier.

"Go away," howled the wind.

"Never!"

Anene climbed up to another spot where a new path zigzagged up the mountain. A heavy burst of rain fell on her, knocking her to the rough ground. Her face fell in a puddle and she coughed heavily after she gasped in water. The fall aggravated every injury from her fight making her cringe in pain. She forced herself up onto her feet, the rains pushing on her as forcefully as a person. "You will not beat me!" She half-walked, half-crawled the path. Rocks tumbling down barely missed her but she continued on. "I am not leaving!"

"Why have you come?" the storm roared. "You are but a mortal. This is not your concern." The wind howled down. "It is not your place."

Anene crawled to the next place that she had to climb. She held her breath and looked up. Through the downpour she could barely make out the top. She was closer, much closer. She found the next handholds. "I'm meant to be your father's bride," she shouted against the storm. The wind suddenly pushed her, knocking a hand free. She swung out over nothing for a moment, her eyes seeing only the world beneath her and her own death. A ragged grunt poured from her as she pulled herself back to the mountain. "Will you kill me too?" she yelled.

The storm died down and Anene took the opportunity to quickly climb as high as she could before the torrent started again. "I should kill you," was the quiet answer.

Anene felt the hate in that statement. "Why would you want me dead? I've done nothing to you."

The rains fell in earnest again and she had to turn her full attention back to climbing. The winds had nothing more to say to her and she had nothing more to say to the goddess of storms. She concentrated on each length climbed, each height achieved. She was nearly knocked off the mountain time and time again, but she dug her fingers into the tiniest cracks and held on. She reached up to what felt like another ledge and pulled herself up and over. She would have laughed if the rains weren't threatening to drown her. Anene looked around to find her next route and saw not just a ledge, but a large flat outcropping. A cave, no, a doorway was carved into the mountainside. She pushed herself to her feet, sliding on the slick stone. Despite the rain and wind, she made her way inside, thankful to be out of the elements. They raged on just beyond the opening, perhaps even harder.

Anene rested against the wall, catching her breath. Water streamed from her, pooling in fat puddles on the floor. She looked farther inside, where low light flickered from another room. She straightened her back, untying her staff from behind her and entered the storm goddess's keep.

♀

The interior of the keep was dark. Torches lit the halls Anene walked down, their light flickering off the smooth walls. She moved cautiously, her staff out. She could run into the storm goddess at any moment. She'd beaten her servant, but wasn't sure if she could fight a goddess. She would try with all her might if it came down to it. Wet footsteps and puddles marked her trail through the mountain and Anene took slight satisfaction at marring the perfect cleanliness of her home.

The halls were spare, without any decoration. The rooms she came to were bare as well. But the thing she noticed most was that the keep was empty. There were no servants, no other gods, not even any animals meandering about. One would think that someone of her importance would have many people wanting to cling to her. But, then again, if her way of greeting people was trying to throw them off her mountain it was understandable why no one came here.

Anene flexed her sore and raw fingers. The climb had worn her down. She knew she needed rest, but not when she was so close to her goal. She just had to figure out how

53

to get the heart away from Sabako. And live. Anene's heart skipped a beat. What if it did come down to a fight? What would she do? Surely the goddess of storms was a terrifying creature. She could command the air itself. What could she hope to counter that kind of power with? Anene shook her head, pushing the thoughts aside. She would figure out something. She had to.

She came to a large antechamber with one tall doorway on the opposite side. Through it muted daylight glowed. Anene crossed the room, her nerves as raw as her hands. She waited for a moment beside the door, listening and trying to calm her heart. She heard nothing, but when she took a chance and glanced in the next room she saw a silhouette near a set of windows. That was her. This was the moment. She closed her eyes, taking three deep breaths, then stepped inside.

She was expecting someone more frightening, someone with a presence that filled the room. Sabako looked barely different than the other gods she'd met. She stood by a series of long windows, looking out to the world. Her hair was only braided halfway, the bottom of her hair as fluffy as clouds. Her skirt was made of volumes of dark gray fabric that moved in a wind that wasn't here. Her feet were bare with dainty toes. Swirling white designs decorated each arm, nearly up to the shoulders, and in those beautiful arms she held the heart.

Anene took a few steps closer, watching in awe as she caressed her father's heart like it was a precious child. Golden blood coated her hands, dripping off her wrists. The storm goddess didn't respond to her presence and Anene didn't know what to say. She swallowed nervously. "Lord

Sabako," she called.

The goddess looked over with sorrowful gray eyes. "I won't let you have it," she said lowly and turned back to the windows.

Anene licked her lips. "Please, allow me to take it back."

"No."

"Please." Sabako didn't respond. "Don't you want to see your father alive again?"

She ran a hand over the heart. "I'd rather have him dead than to share him with you."

Anene stiffened. What had she done to cause such ire in the goddess? "I... I don't know what you mean. Did I do something to offend you, Lord Sabako?"

The goddess cut her eyes at Anene and it was almost like a physical rebuke. "You live."

Anene struggled for words. "I am sorry that my mere life offends you so much." Sabako looked back to the windows. "Great storm goddess," she paused to see if she could get some kind of reaction, "I truly do apologize for whatever it is about me that offends you, but Lord Nniro's heart must be returned." Again, no reaction. Anene held in a frustrated sigh. These gods were infuriating. "If he remains dead, the bounty of the river will stop and my people will die."

"I don't care."

"I will not leave until I have his heart."

Sabako stiffened, cutting her eyes at Anene again. "Your kind are like insects, unwanted and unwelcome. You have sat in my father's house for ages, a stench that could reach even my mountain. At least this way, you won't come between us. Ever again." She held the heart up in her hands. "It will be you and me from now on, father."

Anene didn't respond immediately. Her mind worked to get at the core of this. "Are you jealous?"

"How could I not be?" Her voice grew low and dangerous and the storm clouds outside began to congregate near the windows. "In the beginning I was his whole heart. Now, I have watched him give his heart time and time again to you mortal women. Piece by piece. Little by little. Soon there will be nothing left for me." She brought the heart close to her chest. "I have never understood why he loves you all so much. You're merely his creations. I am his daughter."

Anene stood, astounded. She was behaving like a jealous child. That gods who shaped the world as they pleased could succumb to petty emotions such as this! Anene took a breath. This was ridiculous.

"I can understand how you feel," Anene started slowly. Sabako slid her eyes over, suspicion and hate seeping from them. "I am my parents' only child. My father calls me his shining jewel. I don't think I'd ever accept a new wife if he ever had one." She looked up to the goddess meekly. "But I know he'll love me just as much." She choked up thinking of the parents she may never see again. "I've shared his love with my mother, my grandmother, and the rest of our family. I know there is room in his heart for me and others."

Sabako shook her head. Anene took a step forward. "You hold his heart in your hands," she told the storm goddess. "Surely you can feel his love. Surely you can feel how much he must care for you."

The goddess held the heart up to her lips. She closed her eyes. Sabako's lips moved in words Anene couldn't hear, then a tear roll down her cheek. "I have watched so many of you mortals come and steal him away," she said aloud.

"Lord Sabako, I will be his wife. I could never take away or replace what is in his heart for you."

"But I want it all."

"You can't have it all."

Sabako's mood turned as dark as her storm clouds. "I want it-."

"You can't," Anene snapped. "That's the way it will be. If you cannot accept the simple idea that your father loves you just as much as he did before he took a bride then maybe you don't deserve him. Maybe he is better off dead. He won't have to see his daughter acting so selfishly." Anene struggled to keep her face stern. Her heart felt as if it would beat itself to pieces out of fear. "You killed him out of your jealousy and now hoard his heart because you can't share him with one little mortal woman once a generation. You would let his beloved creations die because you doubt his love for you. Is this how you honor your father? By destroying what he holds dear?"

The storm goddess took a deep breath, looking like a snake preparing to strike. "I...," she started but lost her voice. She looked between Anene and her father's heart for several moments, uncertainty playing across her face. She placed the heart to her lips again. Another tense moment passed. Finally, she sighed. "Take it," she whispered. "Take it. Bring my father back. I want to see his smile again." She held the heart close, one last time, then extended it to Anene.

"Thank you, Lord Sabako," Anene said. She approached the goddess cautiously, still unsure of her. She put her staff on her back and picked up the heart. It was warm and moist in her hands, the blood tingling as it touched her wounds. "Thank you," she said again, bowing as much as she could.

Sabako turned back to the windows. "Be a good wife to him."

"I... will do my best."

Anene tried not to show how elated she was as she left the goddess's presence, but her smile burst through once she walked the hallways. She held the heart in her hands. Anene looked down at it curiously. It was so warm, like it was still in his body. Large enough that it could fill both of her hands, she thought it might start beating at any moment. This was what she needed at long last. She prayed the trip back wouldn't be as eventful as her trip here. But this time, she swore she'd stay on the path. No stopping. No resting until she returned the heart to Nniro.

The rains were gone when Anene stepped outside. Storm clouds still threatened from overhead, but she could see clear down to the foothills. She breathed a sigh of relief and thanked Sabako mentally. She walked to the edge of the plateau, looking over for the best way to start her descent when a shadow passed over her again.

She turned and Obokei landed heavily near her. His face was swollen and near black on one side. One of his shoulders drooped lower than the other. His bloodshot eyes lit with lightning, tiny needles of it racing across his mantle. Anene held the heart to her chest with one arm, pulling out her staff with the other. "Stay away," she said, voice cracking.

He began to walk toward her, a cruel smile on his face as he saw the heart held against her chest. She tried moving to the side, but he stepped in the way. "You have the heart," he said. "What did you do to my lady?"

"Nothing, nothing," she insisted. "We only talked and she-"

"Did you hurt her? Did you?" His voice turned shrill. "I'll make you pay for what you did to me." He was so close Anene had no choice but to back closer to the edge. "And I'll especially make you pay for taking her prize."

Anene swung her staff as best as she could, trying to hit him in the side. He blocked it with his good arm, sending a jolt of electricity down the staff. She cried out in pain and tried to swing again as he reached for her. She missed in her panic. Obokei placed his hand on her shoulder, his smile vanishing, and pushed her from the mountain.

ϙ

Anene felt warm.

She opened her eyes slowly to a blinding golden light. She fell, no, floated in it, and the light embraced her body filling her with a loving warmth. Anene looked at her hands and they were healed. She looked around, twisting awkwardly in mid-air. The gods-world was gone and all she found to look at was the light, then suddenly the figure of her god.

"I'm sorry for all that you've been through," the figure of Nniro said to her. He was just as unearthly beautiful as the rest of the gods, even more so now that she could finally see him alive. Long braids extending to his waist twisted and moved like currents. A host of necklaces made of pearls and shells surrounded his neck. His skirts changed shades of blue moving from light to dark at whim. He smiled at her sadly and Anene felt the sorrow spread through her body. Her eyes threatened to water.

"Where are we?" she asked, starting to panic. "Am I dead?"

"No, dear one." His voice was smooth like the sounds of the river. "We are speaking through my heart." Anene nodded, not sure how to take this odd place.

"I am sorry that such a task had to fall to you, Anene." The loving way he said her name filled her heart. "You have proven to be my fiercest and bravest bride." He reached out a hand to caress her check.

Before she realized what she was doing, she had pulled away. Both she and her patron deity stared at each other in confusion. "Why would you do this to me?"

Nniro's expression turned sorrowful. "It was not my intention for you to have to save me."

"No, why do you have to choose a bride?" She found herself struggling for the right words. "You made us and love us so. You love us so much that your own daughter would steal your heart and cause an entire people to die. But why would you tear a girl away from her home, from everything she knows to be your bride?"

"That is the way your people do it, isn't it? You are sent to your husband's home and may never see your family again."

Anene scowled at him. "But I still may see them. And I would have a new family. His family. Children."

His deep blue eyes pierced her. "It was not my idea to begin to take a bride every generation. I asked your people for a tribute and this is what they decided to give me in return for the river's bounty." When Nniro stroked her cheek this time, she allowed him. "Even though I created humans, I am still in awe of you and your short lives. You take the little that you are born with and do so much. You make the world yours, record its past, sing of its present, and sculpt its future. Forgive me. I only wanted to give one the chance to live the life of a god."

"But no one asked me," she said.

Nniro looked truly confused. "Does... does this trouble you?"

"To my heart." She took her deity's hand and placed it on her chest. "Feel my heart. I didn't want this. I... I want to go home."

He was silent for a moment, his face studying her. "Do you?" his voice rumbled. "Your words conflict with what your heart tells me. Do you really want to go home to all that would be expected of you? Parents that would find you another marriage? A husband that you would grow to despise? Children that you would love out of obligation? I feel your distaste for the very idea of it, Anene."

He placed a hand to her cheek. "I could give you a life of pleasure and see that your every want would be provided for. I would not require you to toil as a mortal wife would or carry children. Wouldn't you rather be with me?"

"But you didn't ask," she insisted. "You didn't ask me or any of the other girls if this is what we wanted."

"Why should I have asked?"

"Because you love us." Nniro looked shocked at her words. "If you love someone, you will at least give them a choice in their lives. Even if my parents chose a man for me, they would at least give me the chance to meet him and see if I liked him. They would choose another if I didn't. You are a god. What choice did I have?"

He looked hurt. "But I wanted to give you everything. My home, my bed, my heart. You would never have to worry about hunger or thirst. You would never feel pain again. Even when you grew old you would never be stooped over or ache. It would be a better life than any mortal could fathom."

Silence passed between them. She sighed. She was beginning to think that Sabako inherited her selfishness. "You owe me."

Nniro didn't answer at first. "I do owe you my life. You have done more for me than any mortal." He looked down, a thoughtful frown across his face. "You have repaid me for your creation. You, Anene, stubborn, brave Anene, have proven yourself greatest of your kind." His face lit up. "You are my greatest creation."

He placed a kiss on her forehead. Anene felt all of his love flood into her and tears began to flow freely down her face. "For you," he said touching his forehead to hers, "I will do anything."

"Anything?"

"Whatever your heart desires." He took a step back from her and his smile melted her heart. "But for now, you must go."

ꝙ

Her fall stopped suddenly and Anene opened her eyes to see Usan staring down at her in concern. He held her tightly and she suddenly felt self-conscious. "Are you all right?" he asked.

She looked to the heart in her hands, still intact, its

blood still over her abused skin. She moved so Usan could let her stand and tested her balance. "I think... I'm fine." She looked up and Sabako's storm-wreathed peak towered over them. She looked to the guardian in amazement. "You caught me. You saved me again. Why?"

"Because I felt your mission, and you, were important."

"Then thank you." She knew she should bow to him but it felt inadequate. She threw her free arm around him in a hug that surprised them both. "Thank you for helping me when so few would."

His voice softened when he replied, "You're welcome." He looked up to the peak and frowned. "Now, let us hurry and return Lord Nniro's heart to him." He took her elbow and ushered her along swiftly.

There was no path ahead of them, but Usan moved with a surety that Anene knew she could trust. The grass-covered foothills seemed to part for them. The large rocks that pointed up toward the mountains shrunk back into the earth. Anene felt swept up in Usan's wake, his speed lending to hers. They walked quickly through a vast grassland, trees shooting up suddenly in the distance then falling away. The larger animals returned, grazing along with their hides in all colors of the rainbow. A predator stalked through the high grass but turned away at their approach, or more likely, Usan's approach.

She looked up to him. "Lord Usan, what are you?"

He glanced back at her. "I am the guardian of the gods-world."

"What... what do you do?"

"I protect it from any wayward mortals that may have come here. I patrol and watch for disturbances." She could tell from his expression that he was searching for the right words. "I am a peacekeeper."

Anene nodded. "Was it your choice? To be the guardian?"

"It is what I was born to do. I have never had any other desire." He glanced back to her quickly and she suddenly felt he was lying.

She sighed. "I wish things were so simple for me."

"What do you desire, Anene?"

The question hit her so sharply. "I... don't know."

Silence passed between them. Only the sounds of passing animals broke it. A pair of birds flew overhead chirping away in conversation. Usan glanced at her again. "Have you thought about the debt Lord Nniro owes you?"

"I spoke with him. When I fell. He said he will do anything for me."

Usan went quiet for a moment. "Will you ask to return home?"

Anene opened her mouth, then closed it. "I'm not sure." Nniro's words haunted her. Did she actually want to return home? What would her reception be? She thought of the terrors on the journey to retrieve the heart. Would she be able to live life not looking over her shoulder every other moment? What kind of daughter would she be to her parents then? And then she would go on to a husband and... children. She frowned at the thought. The idea of bearing and raising children soured her mood. But she could think of no other fate that would await her on the other side.

She looked to Usan. "What do you think I should do?"

The guardian god didn't look back to her when he responded. "That is something I cannot answer for you. You are not the same woman I saw emerge from the Great River. Life with the other mortals I'm sure will feel different to you if you return. I am a god. I have no insight into how a mortal life feels." He paused, slowing down for just a moment. "You must do what you feel is best and what your heart desires. If you do not, you will always live in your past decisions. That much I know for sure."

Anene nodded, falling into her own thoughts as they walked. A jungle soon sprung up around her and the air was filled with the symphony of life. Tree branches swung out of their way respectfully. The flies she'd encountered in her first steps into the gods-world returned, welcoming her back and expressing their relief that she was unharmed. She thanked them reflexively, still lost in thought.

The jungle parted and they stepped back onto the path through a field. Ahead of her she could see the shore of the Great River and across it the hazy shore that must be the world of mortals. The path led down into the river and she could just make out the wavering shape of Nniro's underwater palace. Usan stopped at the spot she'd met him, looking over the river. She stopped beside him, taking a deep breath. Her journey was over.

"You have done more than many would think you were capable of," Usan began, turning those piercing eyes on her. "I had faith that you would make it, but I wasn't sure what condition you would be in when you returned. You have proven yourself brave beyond measure. You should be proud of yourself."

Anene bowed lowly to the god who'd helped her from the start. "Thank you, Lord Usan. I owe so much to you."

He nodded to her. "You are welcome." His lips slowly stretched into a small smile. "I would hope that we would meet again."

"And hopefully not because you have to rescue me." She smiled back and a tiny chuckle escaped him. Anene turned back to the path leading down into Nniro's domain and began her descent.

ꝑ

The trek into the domain of the Great River felt pleasant. The world around her turned cooler, and she felt her weight lessen with the effect of going underwater. The fish that annoyed her on her way out returned, swarming around her. Their large bodies of shimmering, boldly patterned scales circled her closer, rubbing up against her in cold caresses. Anene laughed, her annoyance with them gone. She reached out a hand, stroking their sides, and they felt far softer to the touch than a normal fish. She continued forward, having to keep her eyes down to make sure she was still on the path. Several of the smaller fish nuzzled her cheek and kissed her ears. She laughed at the tickling. It seemed as if they were happy to know their lord was returning.

The school cleared as she drew closer to the compound of Nniro. Anene pressed her free hand to the smooth shell doorway, looking down at the heart she cradled in her arm, and pushed. The door gave way smoothly and she heard a collective gasp as she entered the manor. The fish women servants swam to her, mouths agape as they saw the heart. Many sported red, swollen eyes as if they'd been crying the entire time she was gone.

"My lady," the Jalao began. "How did you do it?"

"That isn't important. What's important is that Nniro and the river live."

The women led her back to Nniro's chambers, the inner doors closed respectfully to conceal their lord's body. She took a deep breath, walking over to the body of the dead god. He lay just as she'd found him, sprawled across the floor by his bed, golden blood pooling. She carefully stepped closer, avoiding the blood on the floor to reach the torn open cavity in his chest.

Her breathing turned heavy, the gravity of the situation settling in on her. She held the heart out at arms length, orienting it correctly. Holding her breath, she lowered the warm mass into his chest and stepped back. Nothing happened at first. Anene leaned in to make sure she had placed it the right way when a light burst from it. The blood on the floor began to draw back to his body. She saw the heart twitch and then give a strong beat that filled the room. The shreds of his chest pulled themselves back together, the lacerations sealing themselves as if nothing had ever marred his skin. All paleness fled his complexion and Nniro's eyes opened.

Anene took a step back as her god stood to his feet. The vision she saw of him could not compare to seeing him before her, alive in his full glory. His hair moved with the water she couldn't feel and he smiled when he laid his eyes on her. Anene swallowed hard and dropped to the floor in supplication. "My lord Nniro."

To her surprise, he dropped to one knee before her. "No, my dearest bride, do not hide your face from me," he said raising her chin. "I thank you with all of my being for what you have done. You have no need to ever prostrate yourself before me again. Please, rise." Anene stood, unsure of what to say to him now that he was truly before her. He led her to an ornate seat made of silver and gold and knelt before her again. "Have you given thought to what I can do for you, dearest Anene?"

Anene swallowed. A host of thoughts ran through her head. There was so much she could ask of him, so much he could do for her and her people. Her people. The sight of them on the shores, singing and cheering her sacrifice came clearly to her mind. "Lord Nniro, will you please not take another bride? Please. Make it clear to the seers that I was to be the last."

Nniro looked surprised at her words then his face settled back into its peaceful smile. "You will be the last chosen. Is there anything else that your heart desires? Anything at all?"

Anene thought furiously. What did she want? Her mother and father's faces floated to the top of her mind and their elation when she'd been chosen. She thought of her friends and her cousins and how they used to play as children. Anene began to open her mouth to speak when Nniro continued.

"Before you answer, I will say this: you are not the same as when you entered the gods-world. Your journey, all that you have survived, has changed you. My spilled blood has mingled with yours." He took her hands, rubbing them and healing the cuts and scrapes. "You are not the same, dearest Anene, and I fear you will never be at peace in the roles a mortal life will place you in now."

Anene looked to her hands. She thought to the animals that meant her harm. She thought to Obokei who tried to kill her. She looked to her god with sorrow in her eyes. He was right. With all that she had gone through, how could she return home? Especially when she didn't want the life that would await her. "Then I will stay here, but I don't wish to be your wife."

Nniro's smile lost some of its brightness but he nodded. "Then what do you wish to be?"

"I wish to have freedom. And I wish to help people."

Nniro rubbed his chin, eyes downcast. Anene wasn't sure if she should have been more specific with her request but those were the two things she wanted most. She didn't want to be tied down to one person, a slave to their whims, god or not, but she still wanted to be able to help people, her people if she could.

He returned his smile to her. Taking both of her hands, he brought her to her feet. "Then my precious Anene, who has saved my life, who braved the wrath of my daughter's mountain - who I'll have a talk with, who traversed the gods-world to bring back the heart of her god to save him and her people, I name you Guardian of the River. Just as you have protected your people and me, so shall you protect the river that connects us."

Nniro placed a hand to her forehead and a golden light enveloped her. Anene gasped. She could feel the divine power enter her, reaching every corner of her being. She felt the waters of the Great River course through her, course out of her, becoming one with her. She could sense schools of fish fleeing fisherman's nets. She heard the sounds of the fisherman and their boats on the waters, heard children splashing in the shallows. She could hear the shouts of women washing clothes and feel the fabrics swaying back and forth in the river.

Nniro lowered his hand and Anene took a deep breath as the light faded. Her skirt had changed. Now it was knee length and made of a sleek material that her hands slid off of. A wreath of necklaces of mother of pearl fell against her chest. Her arms were covered in white, swirling markings similar to those of Nniro. Anene put a hand to her heart. She was changed, truly changed. She felt her new position in the core of her soul and understood her purpose. She lowered her head. "Thank you, Lord Nniro."

Her god took her hands again. "Oh, my greatest creation. Go and enjoy your freedom, free from the expectations of others."

Anene smiled with her whole heart for the first time since coming to the gods-world. "I will."

𐑒

Iselei loved the river. If she could have spent every waking moment in it, swimming, chasing turtles, she would have. She ran out of her family's compound stifling a giggle, or else her grandmother would know she was going out alone. Iselei stopped at the shore taking in the early morning scene. It was beautiful. The sun was just coming up over the trees of the far shore making the waters look like liquid gold. Birds flew low, spearing fish on the wing. Iselei mimicked their calls, sending them into confused flight patterns.

She laughed, happily stripping off her clothes and kicking her shoes to the side. She shivered as she took the first step into the river. The cool waters swirled around her ankles and the underwater plants tickled her feet. Iselei waded out farther, splashing herself to get used to the temperature. She looked to the other shore as she splashed. Curiosity pricked her about the other side. She wondered if there were the same plants and animals as here. She was a strong swimmer. She knew that, but could she make it that far? Fear brushed her for a moment but was replaced by childish hubris. There was only one way to find out.

Iselei waded out until the waters reached her neck and each step made her bounce along. With a giant smile, she began to swim. She took confident strokes. She wanted to know what sorts of fish she'd see in the middle of the river, just as much as she wanted to see the other side. There had to be giant ones out there. Maybe even fish as big as she was long. Iselei glanced back and her village was farther than it had ever been. Fear tried to rise but she ignored it. She'd be back soon enough.

A few more minutes and her arms started to tire. Iselei took a moment to rest, floating in the deep waters. She looked back to her shore and it seemed a world away. She looked to the far side in despair. She wasn't even halfway there yet. She didn't think she could make it. Iselei sighed deeply. One goal floated away like a leaf on the current.

Near her a fishing bird landed. It looked at her curiously then dived quickly under the surface. Iselei's eyes lit up. If she couldn't reach the other shore, then maybe she could reach the bottom. If a bird could do it then surely she could. She took a deep breath and sunk beneath the waters.

It was murkier than she thought it would be. She saw the bird swimming down ahead of her and followed. It was like a game. Where the bird changed direction, so did she. She finally stopped when it started to dart around to catch a fish. Iselei worked against the current to continue watching and before she knew it her lungs began burning. She turned to swim back to the surface and the sunshine seemed so far away.

Panic descended on her. This was a horrible idea. She swam as fast as her limbs could move but the surface was still out of her reach. She was going to drown. Her body finally betrayed her, and she opened her mouth to take a breath. She fought as river water rushed into her lungs. The surface was farther away than she thought. The light of the sun started to grow dimmer.

Arms suddenly wrapped around her. Iselei was turned around to face a woman who looked like she could be any of her cousins or sisters. The woman kissed her and suddenly she could breathe. With a smile the woman helped her to the surface, moving quicker than any human swimmer should be able to.

They broke the surface and Iselei realized that they were in the shallows. She struggled to her hands and knees, thankful to be on land again. She looked behind her and caught one last glimpse of the woman's smile before she disappeared below the waters. Iselei jumped to her feet, snatching up her clothes and sandals. "Mama!" she shouted, running as fast as she could to her home. "I saw her! I saw the guardian!"

SARAH A. MACKLIN is a writer born and raised just outside of Columbia, SC. She has written several short stories that have appeared in FIYAH Literary Magazine, The Magazine of Fantasy and Science Fiction, Translunar Traveler's Lounge, and the *Griots: Sisters of the Spear* anthology. Her debut novel, *The Royal Heretic*, was released in 2020. When not writing prose, you can find her working on comics or at her sewing machine busy with a new outfit. She resides just beyond the outskirts of suburbia with her husband and two daughters.